THIS BOOK BELONGS TO

....

100 Poems for Children

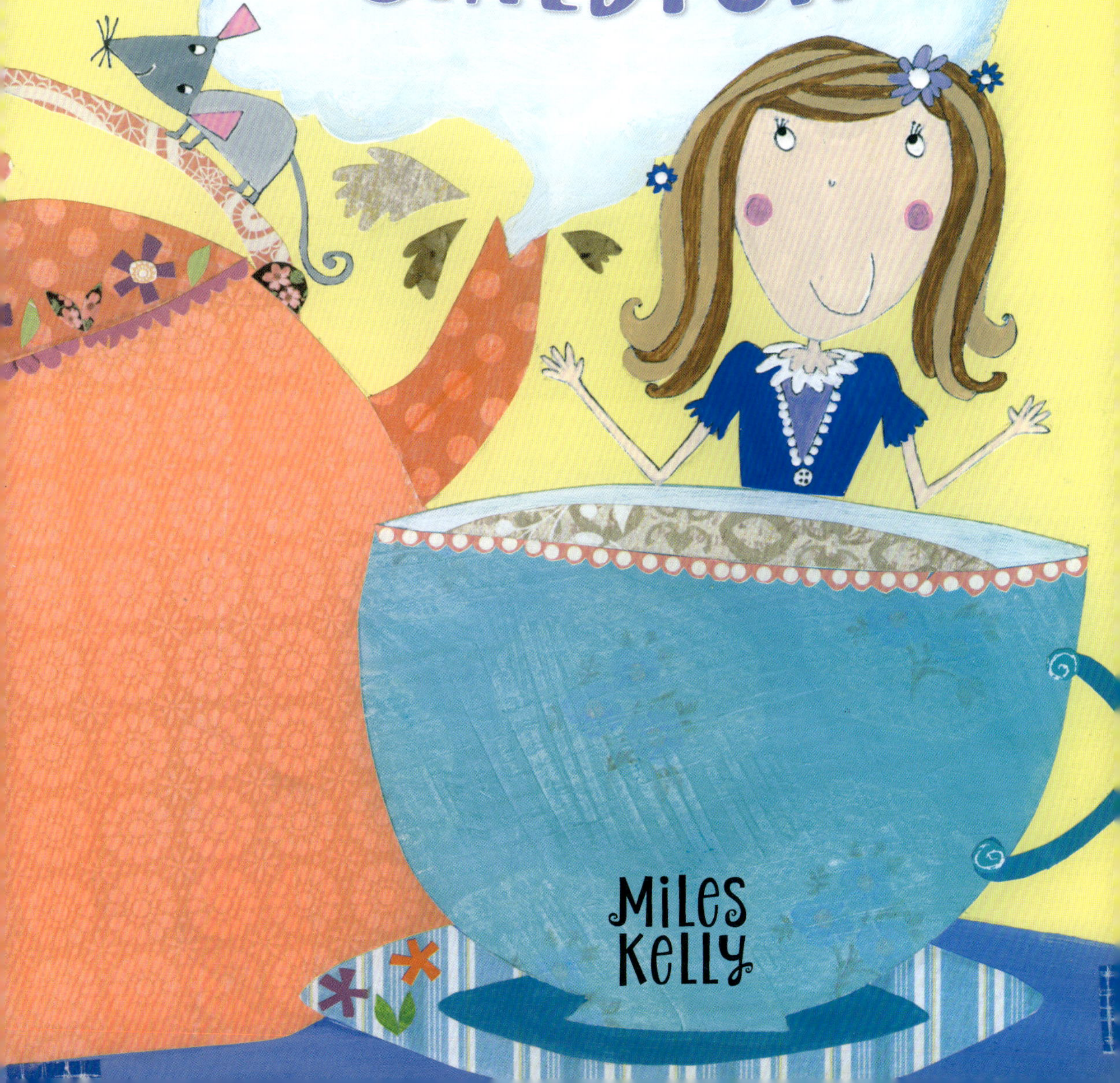

Miles Kelly

First published in 2021 by Miles Kelly Publishing Ltd
Harding's Barn, Bardfield End Green, Thaxted, Essex, CM6 3PX, UK

2 4 6 8 10 9 7 5 3 1

Publishing Director Belinda Gallagher
Creative Director Jo Cowan
Editorial Director Rosie Neave
Senior Editor Becky Miles
Cover Designer Jo Cowan
Design Manager Simon Lee
Image Manager Liberty Newton
Production Controller Jennifer Brunwin
Reprographics Stephan Davis
Assets Lorraine King

Cover Artist Sue Reeves, The Bright Agency
All artwork from the Miles Kelly Artwork Bank

ISBN 978-1-78989-229-1

Printed in China

British Library Cataloguing-in-Publication Data
A catalogue record for this book is available from the British Library

Made with paper from a sustainable forest

www.mileskelly.net

Contents

This book is a treasure trove of words, full of delightful poetry to suit all moods. Some poems are very old, but they speak of experiences that anyone can understand, such as having a cold nose in winter or chasing butterflies in the garden.

Fun and Nonsense

TOAD

The Owl and the Pussy-cat

The Owl and the Pussy-cat went to sea
In a beautiful pea-green boat,
They took some honey, and plenty of money,
Wrapped up in a five-pound note.
The Owl looked up to the stars above,
And sang to a small guitar,
"Oh, lovely Pussy, oh, Pussy, my love,
What a beautiful Pussy you are,
You are,
You are!
What a beautiful Pussy you are!"

Pussy said to the Owl,
  "You elegant fowl,
  How charmingly sweet you sing!
Oh, let us be married;
  too long we have tarried:
  But what shall we do for a ring?"
They sailed away for a year and a day,
  To the land where the bong-tree grows;
And there in the wood a Piggy-wig stood,
  With a ring at the end of his nose,
    His nose,
    His nose,
  With a ring at the end of his nose.

"Dear Pig, are you willing to sell for one shilling
Your ring?" Said the Piggy, "I will."
So they took it away and were married next day
By the Turkey who lives on the hill.
They dined on mince and slices of quince,
Which they ate with a runcible spoon;
And hand in hand, on the edge of the sand,
They danced by the light of the moon,
The moon,
The moon,
They danced by the light of the moon.

Edward Lear

Betty Botter Bought some Butter

Betty Botter bought some butter,
But, she said, this butter's bitter;
If I put it in my batter
It will make my batter bitter.
But a bit of better butter
Will make my batter better.

So she bought a bit of butter
Better than her bitter butter,
And she put it in her batter
And the batter was not bitter.
So, 'twas better Betty Botter
Bought a bit of better butter.

Anonymous

The Cats have Come to Tea

What did she see – oh, what did she see,
As she stood leaning against the tree?
Why all the cats had come to tea.

What a fine turn out –
from round about,
All the houses had let them out,
And here they were with
scamper and shout.

"Mew-mew-mew!" was all they could say,
And, "We hope we find you well today."

Mew-mew-mew!

Oh, what should she do – oh, what should she do?
What a lot of milk they would get through;
For here they were with "Mew-mew-mew!"

She didn't know – oh, she didn't know,
If bread and butter they'd like or no;
They might want little mice, oh! oh! oh!

Dear me – oh, dear me,
All the cats had come to tea.

Kate Greenaway

Amelia

Amelia mixed the mustard,
She mixed it good and thick:
She put it in the custard
And made her Mother sick,
And showing satisfaction
By many a loud huzza,
"Observe," said she, "the action
Of mustard on Mamma."

A E Housman

Why?

There was a young maid who said, "Why
Can't I look in my ear with my eye?
If I give my mind to it,
I'm sure I can do it,
You never can tell till you try."

Anonymous

The Triantiwontigongolope

There's a very funny insect that you do not often spy,
And it isn't quite a spider, and it isn't quite a fly;
It is something like a beetle, and a little like a bee,
But nothing like a woolly grub that climbs upon a tree.
Its name is quite a hard one, but you'll learn it soon, I hope.
So try:

"Tri-
Tri-anti-wonti-
Triantiwontigongolope"

Beetle-bee

Spider-fly

It lives on weeds and wattle-gum, and has a funny face;
Its appetite is hearty, and its manners a disgrace.
When first you come upon it, it will give you quite a scare,
But when you look for it again, you find it isn't there.
And unless you call it softly it will stay away and mope.

So try:

"TRI-
TRI-anti-wonti-
TRIantiwontigongoLOPE"

Wattle-gum: a sticky substance from the trunk of the wattle tree

It trembles if you tickle it or tread upon its toes;
It is not an early riser, but it has a snubbish nose.
If you snear at it, or scold it, it will scuttle off in shame,
But it purrs and purrs quite proudly if you call it by its name,
And offer it some sandwiches of sealing-wax and soap.
So try:

"TRI-
TRI-anti-wonti-
Triantiwontigongolope"

 Sealing-wax: a stiff wax used to seal an envelope

But of course you haven't seen it; and I truthfully confess
That I haven't seen it either, and I don't know its address.
For there isn't such an insect, though there really
might have been
If the trees and grass were purple, and the sky
was bottle green.
It's just a little joke of mine, which you'll forgive, I hope.
Oh, try!
"TRI-
TRI-anti-wonti-
TRiantiwontigongolope"

C J Dennis

From

Topsy Turvy World

If the butterfly courted the bee,
And the owl the porcupine;
If the churches were built in the sea,
And three times one was nine;
If the pony rode his master,
If the buttercups ate the cows,
If the cat had the dire disaster
To be worried, sir, by the mouse;
If any or all of these wonders
Should ever come about,
I should not consider them blunders,
For I should be inside out!

William Brighty Rands

The Man with the Beard

There was an Old Man with a beard,
Who said, "It is just as I feared! –
Two owls and a hen,
Four larks and a wren,
Have all built their nests in my beard!"

Edward Lear

Wouldn't it be Funny?

Wouldn't it *be* funny –
Wouldn't it, now –
If the dog said, "Moo-oo"
And the cow said, "Bow-wow"?
If the cat sang and whistled,
And the bird said, "Mia-ow"?
Wouldn't it *be* funny –
Wouldn't it, now?

Anonymous

Mia-ow! Mia-ow!
Mia-ow! Mia-ow!

Bow-wow!
Bow-wow!

Moo-oo! Moo-oo!
Moo-oo! Moo-oo!

Calico Pie

Calico Pie,
The little Birds fly
Down to the calico tree,
Their wings were blue,
And they sang "Tilly-loo!"
Till away they flew, –
And they never came back to me!
They never came back!
They never came back!
They never came back to me!

Calico Jam,
The little Fish swam,
Over the syllabub sea,
He took off his hat,
To the Sole and the Sprat,
And the Willeby-Wat, –
But he never came back to me!
He never came back!
He never came back!
He never came back to me!

Calico Ban,
The little Mice ran,
To be ready in time for tea,
Flippity flup,
They drank it all up,
And danced in the cup, –
But they never came back to me!
They never came back!
They never came back!
They never came back to me!

Calico Drum,
The Grasshoppers come,
The Butterfly, Beetle, and Bee,
Over the ground,
Around and around,
With a hop and a bound, –
But they never came back to me!
They never came back!
They never came back!
They never came back to me!

Edward Lear

A Big Shoe

Said little Sue
To little Pete,
"I can't see you,
For your big feet."

Said little Pete
To little Sue
"'Tis not my feet,
'Tis but my shoe."

Anonymous

Tweedledum and Tweedledee

Tweedledum and Tweedledee
Resolved to have a battle
For Tweedledum said Tweedledee
Had spoiled his nice new rattle.

Just then flew by a monstrous crow
As big as a tar barrel,
Which frightened both the heroes so
They quite forgot their quarrel.

Anonymous

Jabberwocky

'Twas brillig, and the slithy toves
Did gyre and gimble in the wabe;
All mimsy were the borogoves,
And the mome raths outgrabe.

"Beware the Jabberwock, my son!
The jaws that bite, the claws that catch!
Beware the Jubjub bird, and shun
The frumious Bandersnatch!"

He took his vorpal sword in hand:
Long time the manxome
foe he sought.
So rested he by
the Tumtum tree,
And stood awhile in
thought.

This poem sounds as if it is full of difficult words, but most of them are made up; they can mean whatever you want them to mean.

And as in uffish thought he stood,
The Jabberwock with eyes of flame,
Came whiffling through the tulgey wood,
And burbled as it came!

One, two! One, two! And through, and through
The vorpal blade went snicker-snack!
He left it dead, and with its head
He went galumphing back.

"And hast thou slain the Jabberwock?
Come to my arms, my beamish boy!
Oh, frabjous day! Callooh! Callay!"
He chortled in his joy.

'Twas brillig, and the slithy toves
Did gyre and gimble in the wabe;
All mimsy were the borogoves
And the mome raths outgrabe.

Lewis Carroll

The Old Man in a Tree

There was an Old Man in a tree
Who was horribly bored by a bee;
When they said, "Does it buzz?"
He replied, "Yes, it does!
It's a regular brute of a bee!"

Edward Lear

Jerry Hall

Jerry Hall, he was so small,
A rat could eat him, hat and all.

Anonymous

The Young Person in Green

There was a Young Person in green,
Who seldom was fit to be seen;
She wore a long shawl, over bonnet and all,
Which enveloped that person in green.

Edward Lear

The Person of Ware

There was an Old Person of Ware,
Who rode on the back of a bear;
When they asked, "Does it trot?"
he said, "Certainly not!
He's a Moppsikon Floppsikon bear!"

Edward Lear

Edward Lear loved inventing nonsense words such as 'moppsikon floppsikon' – he never explained their meaning.

There was an Old Lady

There was an old lady who swallowed a fly
I don't know why she swallowed a fly –
perhaps she'll die!

There was an old lady who swallowed a spider,
That wriggled and wiggled and tickled inside her,
She swallowed the spider to catch the fly;
I don't know why she swallowed a fly –
perhaps she'll die!

There was an old lady who swallowed a bird;
How absurd to swallow a bird.
She swallowed the bird to catch the spider,
She swallowed the spider to catch the fly;
I don't know why she swallowed a fly –
perhaps she'll die!

There was an old lady who swallowed a cat;
Fancy that to swallow a cat!
She swallowed the cat to catch the bird,
She swallowed the bird to catch the spider,
She swallowed the spider to catch the fly;
I don't know why she swallowed a fly –
perhaps she'll die!

There was an old lady who swallowed a dog;
What a hog, to swallow a dog;
She swallowed the dog to catch the cat,
She swallowed the cat to catch the bird,
She swallowed the bird to catch the spider,
She swallowed the spider to catch the fly;
I don't know why she swallowed a fly –
perhaps she'll die!

There was an old lady who swallowed a cow,
I don't know how she swallowed a cow;
She swallowed the cow to catch the dog,
She swallowed the dog to catch the cat,
She swallowed the cat to catch the bird,
She swallowed the bird to catch the spider,
She swallowed the spider to catch the fly;
I don't know why she swallowed a fly –
perhaps she'll die!

There was an old lady who swallowed a horse,
She's dead, of course!

Anonymous

The Young Lady of Norway

There was a Young Lady of Norway,
Who casually sat in a doorway;
When the door squeezed her flat,
she exclaimed, "What of that?"
This courageous Young Lady of Norway.

Edward Lear

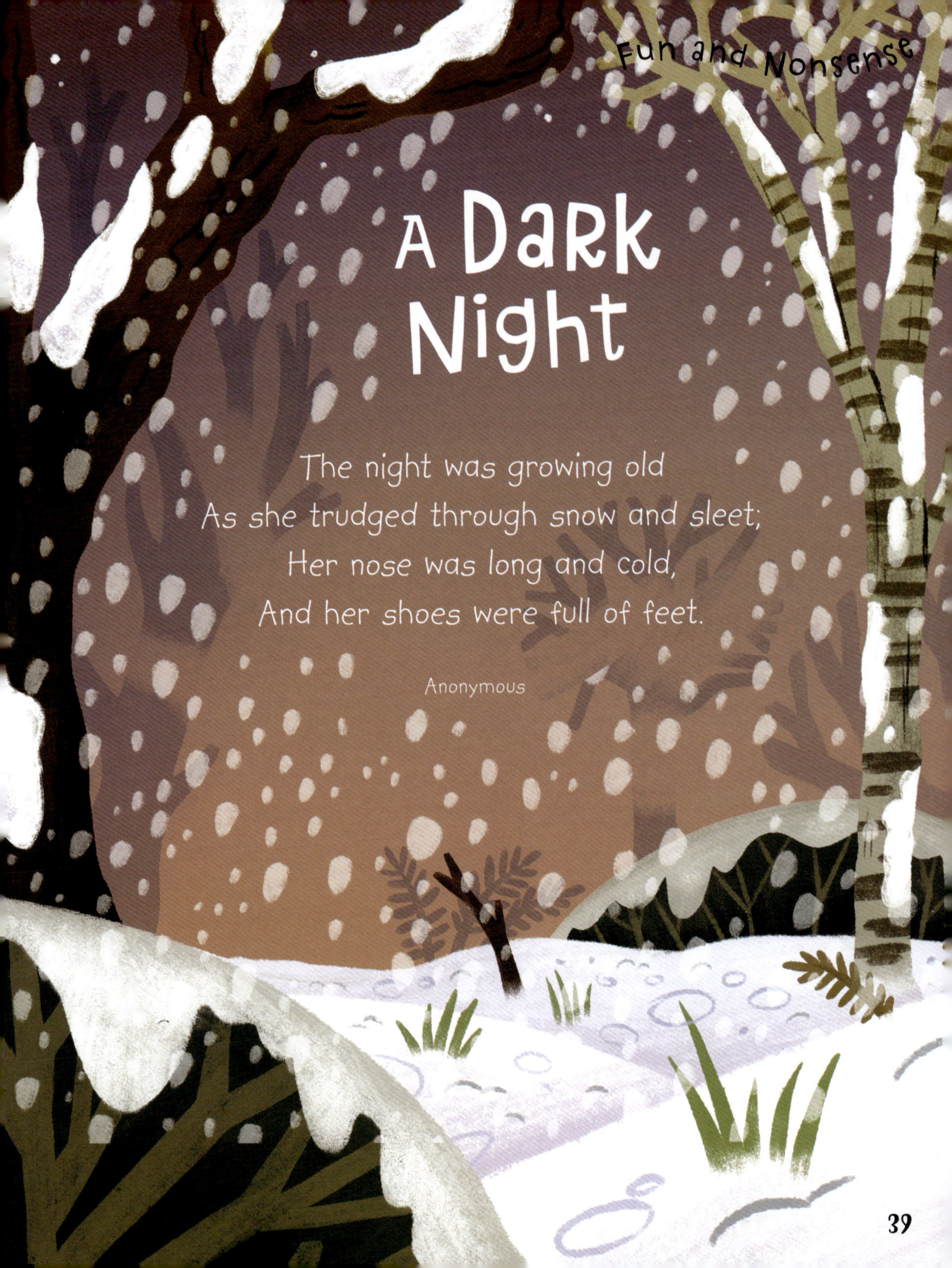

A Dark Night

The night was growing old
As she trudged through snow and sleet;
Her nose was long and cold,
And her shoes were full of feet.

Anonymous

Mr Toad

The world has held great Heroes,
As history-books have showed;
But never a name to go down to fame
Compared with that of Toad!

The clever men at Oxford
Know all that there is to be knowed.
But they none of them know one half as much
As intelligent Mr Toad!

The animals sat in the Ark and cried,
Their tears in torrents flowed.
Who was it said, "There's land ahead?"
Encouraging Mr Toad!

The army all saluted
As they marched along the road.
Was it the King? Or Kitchener?
No. It was Mr Toad.

The Queen and her Ladies-in-waiting
Sat at the window and sewed.
She cried, "Look! Who's that HANDSOME man?"
They answered, "Mr Toad."

Kenneth Grahame

The Music of Your Voice

A vase upon the mantelpiece,
  A ship upon the sea,
A goat upon a mountain-top
  Are much the same to me;
But when you mention melon jam,
  Or picnics by the creek,
Or apple pies, or pantomimes,
  I love to hear you speak.

The date of Magna Carta or
The doings of the Dutch,
Or capes, or towns, or verbs, or nouns
Do not excite me much;
But when you mention motor rides –
Down by the sea for choice
Or chasing games, or chocolates,
I love to hear your voice.

C J Dennis

Magna Carta: an important document signed by the King of England in 1215

All the Day Long

Good Morning

The year's at the Spring,
And day's at the morn;
Morning's at seven;
The hillside's dew-pearled;
The lark's on the wing;
The snail's on the thorn;
God's in his heaven –
All's right with the world.

Robert Browning

Three Little Rules

Three little rules we all should keep.
To make life happy and bright.

Smile in the morning, smile at noon.
And keep on smiling at night.

Anonymous

My Shadow

I have a little shadow that goes in and out with me,
And what can be the use of him is more than I can see.
He is very, very like me from the heels up to the head;
And I see him jump before me, when I jump into my bed.

The funniest thing about him is
 the way he likes to grow –
Not at all like proper children,
 which is always very slow;
For he sometimes shoots up taller
 like an india-rubber ball,
And he sometimes goes so little that
 there's none of him at all.

He hasn't got a notion of how children ought to play,
And can only make a fool of me in every sort of way.
He stays so close behind me, he's a coward you can see;
I'd think shame to stick to nursie as that shadow
sticks to me!

One morning, very early,
before the sun was up,
I rose and found the shining dew
on every buttercup;
But my lazy little shadow,
like an arrant sleepy-head,
Had stayed at home behind me
and was fast asleep in bed.

Robert Louis Stevenson

Nursie: a nanny
Arrant: complete

Little Things

Little drops of water,
Little grains of sand,
Make the mighty ocean
And the pleasant land.
Little deeds of kindness,
Little words of love,
Make our world an Eden
Like the Heaven above.

Julia Carney

Arabella Miller

Little Arabella Miller
Had a fuzzy caterpillar.
First it climbed upon her mother,
Then upon her *baby* brother.
They said, "Arabella Miller,
Put away your caterpillar!"

Anonymous

Hair Brushing

One for a tangle,
One for a curl,
One for a boy
And one for a girl,
One to make a parting,
One to tie a bow,
One to blow the cobwebs out
And one to make it grow.

Anonymous

From

Poem to her Daughter

Daughter, take this amulet,
tie it with cord and caring.
I'll make you a chain of coral and pearl
to glow on your neck. I'll dress you nobly.
A gold clasp too – fine, without flaw,
to keep with you always.
When you bathe, sprinkle perfume,
  and weave your hair in braids,
string jasmine for the counterpane.
Wear your clothes like a bride,
anklets for your feet, bracelets for your arms...
Don't forget rosewater,
don't forget henna for the palms of your hands...

Mwana Kupona binti Msham

Amulet: a charm to keep the wearer safe
Henna: a reddish-brown dye

This poem was originally written in the African language Swahili by a Kenyan woman in the 19th century.

Quick, Quick

Quick, quick
The cat's been sick
Where, where?
Under the chair.
Hasten, hasten
Fetch a basin.
Too late, too late,
'Tis all in vain,
The cat has licked it
Up again.

Anonymous

Jelly

Jelly on the plate
Jelly on the plate
Wibble wobble
Wibble wobble
Jelly on the plate.

Anonymous

From

A Boy's Aspiration

I was four yesterday – when I'm quite old,
I'll have a cricket-ball made of pure gold;
I'll carve the roast meat, and help soup and fish;
I'll get my feet wet whenever I wish;

I'll spend a hundred pounds every day;
I'll have the alphabet quite done away;
I'll have a parrot without a sharp beak;
I'll see a pantomime six times a week;

I'll never stand up to show that I'm grown;
No one shall say to me, "Don't throw a stone!"
I'll drop my butter'd toast on the new chintz;
I'll have no governess giving her hints.

Chintz: patterned fabric used for sofas, chairs and curtains

I'll have a nursery up in the stars;
I'll lean through windows without any bars;
I'll sail without my nurse in a big boat;
I'll have no comforters tied round my throat;

I'll have a language with not a word spell'd;
I'll ride on horseback without being held;
I'll hear Mamma say, "My boy, good as gold!"
When I'm a grown-up man sixty years old.

Menella Bute Smedley

My Books

I love my books
They are the homes
of queens and fairies,
Knights and gnomes.

Each time I read I make a call
On some quaint person large or small,
Who welcomes me with hearty hand
And leads me through his wonderland.

Each book is like
A city street
Along whose winding way I meet
New friends and old who laugh and sing
And take me off adventuring!

Anonymous

A Little Song of Life

Glad that I live am I;
That the sky is blue;
Glad for the country lanes,
And the fall of dew.

After the sun the rain;
After the rain the sun;
This is the way of life,
Till the work be done.

All that we need to do,
Be we low or high,
Is to see that we grow
Nearer the sky.

Lizette Woodworth Reese

A Kiss when I Wake

A kiss when I wake in the morning
A kiss when I go to bed,
A kiss when I burn my fingers,
A kiss when I bump my head.
A kiss when my bath begins
A kiss when my bath is over,
My mamma is as full of kisses
As nurse is full of pins.
A kiss when I play with my rattle;
A kiss when I pull her hair,
She covered me all over with kisses
The day that I fell down stair.
A kiss when I give her trouble,
A kiss when I give her joy;
There's nothing like mamma's kisses
To her own little baby boy.

Anonymous

At the Zoo

First I saw the white bear, then I saw the black;
Then I saw the camel with a hump upon his back;
Then I saw the grey wolf, with mutton in his maw;
Then I saw the wombat waddle in the straw;
Then I saw the elephant a-waving of his trunk;
Then I saw the monkeys – mercy, how
unpleasantly they – smelt!

William Makepeace Thackeray

Maw: mouth

Dog Problems

Our dog Fred
Et the bread.

Our dog Pete
Et the meat.

Our dog Davy
Et the gravy.

Our dog Toffee
Et the coffee.

Our dog Jake
Et the cake.

Our dog Trip
Et the dip.

And – the worst,
From the first, –

Our dog Fido
Et the pie-dough.

James Whitcomb Riley

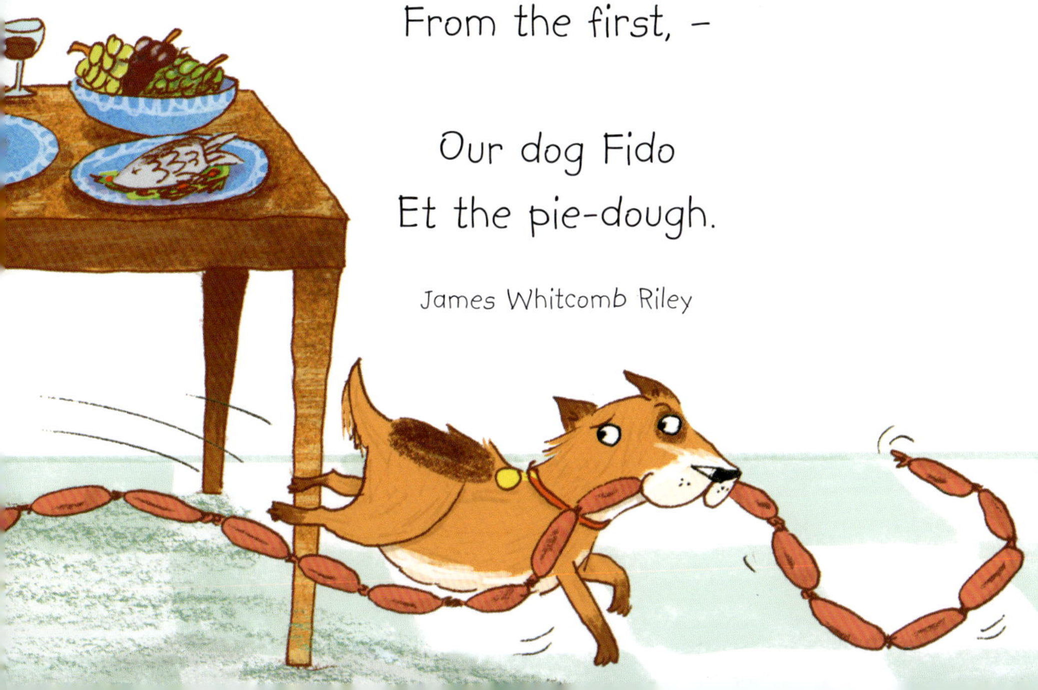

Wash the Dishes

Wash the dishes,
Wipe the dishes,
Ring the bell for tea.

Three good wishes,
Three good kisses,
I will give to thee.

Anonymous

Apples

An apple a day
Sends the doctor away
Apple in the morning
Doctor's warning
Roast apple at night
Starves the doctor outright
Eat an apple going to bed
Knock the doctor on the head.

Anonymous

The Ferry of Shadowtown

Sway to and fro in the twilight grey;
This is the ferry for Shadowtown;
It always sails at the end of the day,
Just as the darkness closes down.

Rest, little head, on my shoulder so
A sleepy kiss is the only fare;
Drifting away from the world we go,
Baby and I in the rocking chair.

See, where the fire logs glow and spark,
Glitter the lights of the shadowland;
The raining drops on the window, hark!
Are ripples lapping upon its strand.

There, where the mirror is glancing dim,
A lake lies shimmering, cool and still;
Blossoms are waving above its brim,
Those over there on the window sill.

Rock slow, more slow, in the dusky light,
Silently lower the anchor down,
Dear little passenger, say "Good night!"
We've reached the harbour for Shadowtown!

Ethelbert Nevin

Strand: shore

A Good Play

We built a ship upon the stairs
All made of the back-bedroom chairs,
And filled it full of sofa pillows
To go a-sailing on the billows.

We took a saw and several nails,
And water in the nursery pails;
And Tom said, "Let us also take
An apple and a slice of cake;"
Which was enough for Tom and me
To go a-sailing on, till tea.

We sailed along for days and days,
And had the very best of plays;
But Tom fell out and hurt his knee,
So there was no one left but me.

Robert Louis Stevenson

At the Seaside

When I was down beside the sea
A wooden spade they gave to me
To dig the sandy shore.
My holes were empty like a cup.
In every hole the sea came up,
Till it could come no more.

Robert Louis Stevenson

From

Night

The sun descending in the west,
The evening star does shine;
The birds are silent in their nest,
And I must seek for mine.
The moon like a flower,
In heaven's high bower,
With silent delight
Sits and smiles on the night.

William Blake

Little Fishes in a Brook

Little fishes in a brook,
Father caught them on a hook,
Mother fried them in a pan,
Johnnie eats them like a man.

Anonymous

The Lamplighter

My tea is nearly ready
  and the sun has left the sky.
It's time to take the window
  to see Leerie going by;
For every night at teatime
  and before you take your seat,
With lantern and with ladder
  he comes posting up the street.

Now Tom would be a driver
  and Maria go to sea,
And my papa's a banker
  and as rich as he can be;
But I, when I am stronger
  and can choose what I'm to do,
O Leerie, I'll go round at night
  and light the lamps with you!

For we are very lucky,
with a lamp before the door,
And Leerie stops to light it
as he lights so many more;
And oh! before you hurry by
with ladder and with light;
O Leerie, see a little child
and nod to him tonight!

Robert Louis Stevenson

Street lamps used to be lit by gas, and a lamplighter had to light each one.

Young Night-thought

All night long and every night,
When my mama puts out the light,
I see the people marching by,
As plain as day before my eye.

Armies and emperor and kings,
All carrying different kinds of things,
And marching in so grand a way,
You never saw the like by day.

So fine a show was never seen
At the great circus on the green;
For every kind of beast and man
Is marching in that caravan.

As first they move a little slow,
But still the faster on they go,
And still beside me close I keep
Until we reach the town of Sleep.

Robert Louis Stevenson

Caravan: group of people travelling together

Bedtime in Summer

In winter I get up at night
And dress by yellow candle-light.
In summer quite the other way,
I have to go to bed by day.

I have to go to bed and see
The birds still hopping on the tree,
Or hear the grown-up people's feet
Still going past me in the street.

And does it not seem hard to you,
When all the sky is clear and blue,
And I should like so much to play,
To have to go to bed by day?

Robert Louis Stevenson

A Good Boy

I woke before the morning, I was happy all the day,
I never said an ugly word, but smiled and stuck to play.

And now at last the sun is going down behind the wood,
And I am very happy, for I know that I've been good.

My bed is waiting cool and fresh, with linen smooth and fair,
And I must be off to sleepsin-by, and not forget my prayer.

I know that, till tomorrow I shall see the sun arise,
No ugly dream shall fright my mind, no ugly sight my eyes.

But slumber hold me tightly till I waken in the dawn,
And hear the thrushes singing in the lilacs round the lawn.

Robert Louis Stevenson

Tumbling

In jumping and tumbling
We spend the whole day,
Till night by arriving
Has finished our play.
What then? One and all,
There's no more to be said,
As we tumbled all day,
So we tumble to bed.

Anonymous

My Bed is a Boat

My bed is like a little boat;
Nurse helps me in when I embark;
She girds me in my sailor's coat
And starts me in the dark.

At night I go on board and say
Goodnight to all my friends on shore;
I shut my eyes and sail away
And see and hear no more.

And sometimes things to bed I take,
As prudent sailors have to do;
Perhaps a slice of wedding-cake,
Perhaps a toy or two.

All night across the dark we steer;
But when the day returns at last,
Safe in my room beside the pier,
I find my vessel fast.

Robert Louis Stevenson

Gird: to wrap up

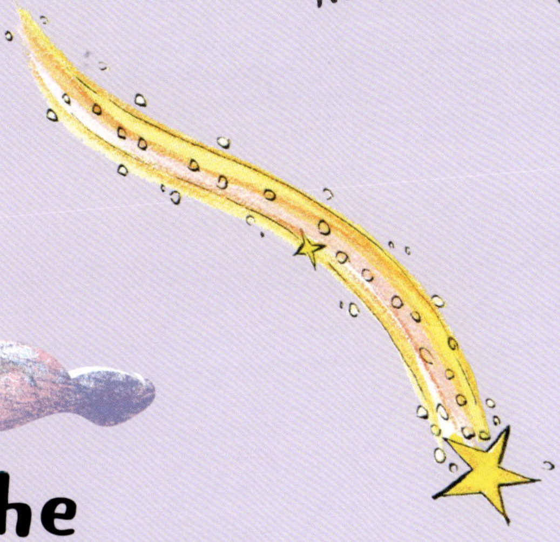

The Falling Star

I saw a star slide down the sky,
Blind the north as it went by,
Too burning and too quick to hold,
Too lovely to be bought or sold,
Good only to make wishes on
And then forever to be gone.

Sara Teasdale

Wonderful World

Caterpillar

Brown and furry
Caterpillar in a hurry,
Take your walk
To the shady leaf, or stalk,
Or what not,
Which may be the chosen spot.
No toad spy you,
Hovering bird of prey pass by you;
Spin and die,
To live again a butterfly.

Christina Rossetti

Hurt no Living Thing

Hurt no living thing:
Ladybird, nor butterfly,
Nor moth with dusty wing,
Nor cricket chirping cheerily,
Nor grasshopper so light of leap,
Nor dancing gnat, nor beetle fat,
Nor harmless worms that creep.

Christina Rossetti

White Sheep

White sheep, white sheep,
On a blue hill,
When the wind stops
You all stand still.

When the wind blows,
You walk away slow.
White sheep, white sheep,
Where do you go?

Anonymous

This could be a poem about sheep, but it might also be about the sky and clouds.

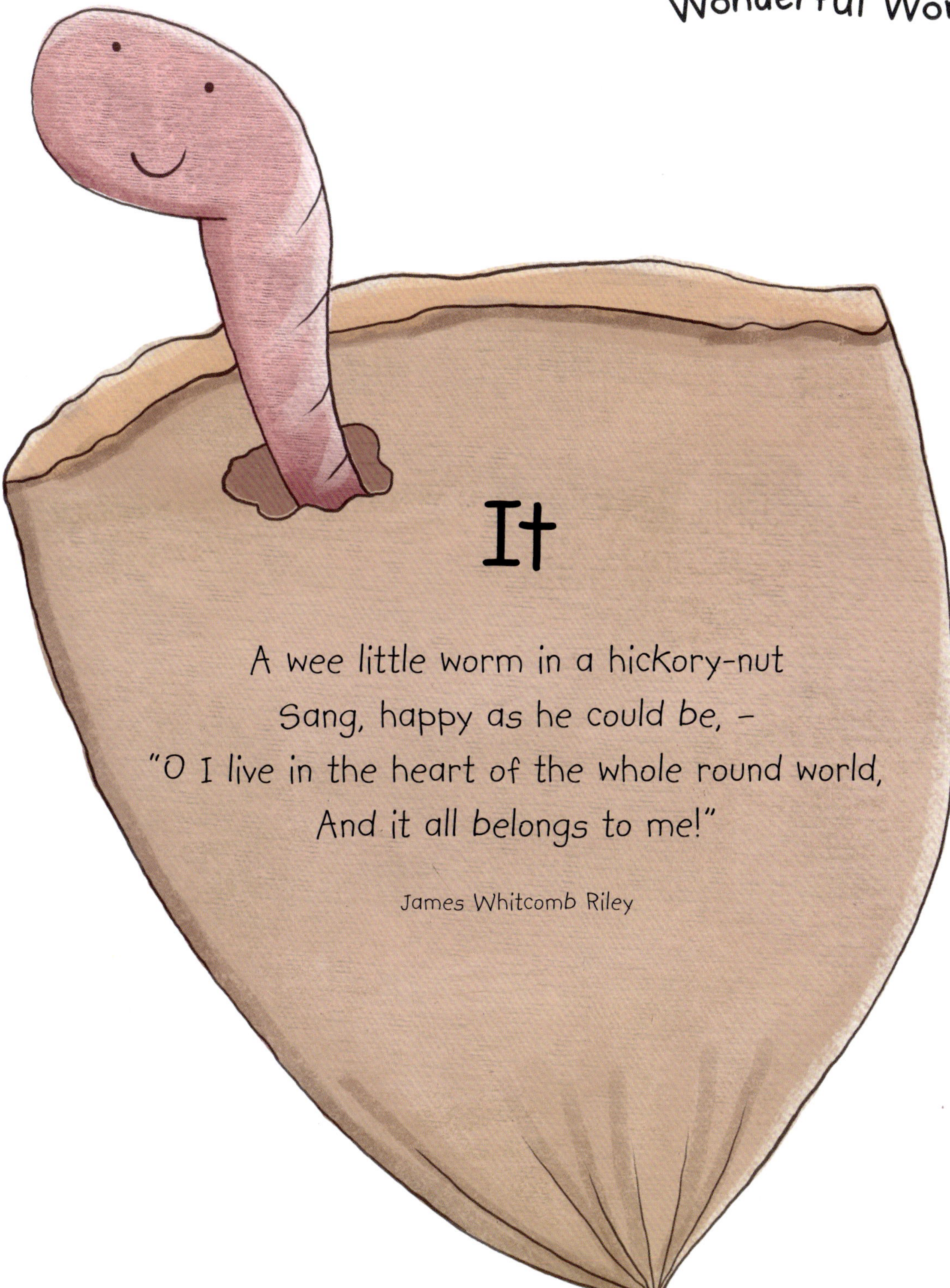

It

A wee little worm in a hickory-nut
Sang, happy as he could be, –
"O I live in the heart of the whole round world,
And it all belongs to me!"

James Whitcomb Riley

From

Strange Meetings

The stars must make an awful noise
In whirling round the sky;
Yet somehow I can't even hear
Their loudest song or sigh.

So it is wonderful to think
One blackbird can outsing
The voice of all the swarming stars
On any day in Spring.

Harold Monro

November Night

Listen...
With faint dry sound,
Like steps of passing ghosts,
The leaves, frost-crisp'd, break from the trees
And fall.

Adelaide Crapsey

All the Year Round

January brings the snow,
makes our feet and fingers glow.

February brings the rain,
Thaws the frozen lake again.

March brings breezes loud and shrill,
stirs the dancing daffodil.

April brings the primrose sweet,
Scatters daises at our feet.

May brings flocks of pretty lambs,
Skipping by their fleecy dams.

June brings tulips, lilies, roses,
Fills the children's hands with posies.

Hot **July** brings cooling showers,
Apricots and gillyflowers.

August brings the sheaves of corn,
Then the harvest home is borne.

Warm **September** brings the fruit,
Sportsmen then begin to shoot.

Fresh **October** brings the pheasants,
Then to gather nuts is pleasant.

Dull **November** brings the blast,
Then the leaves are whirling fast.

Chill **December** brings the sleet,
Blazing fire, and Christmas treat.

Sara Coleridge

Gillyflowers: carnations

The Wind has such a Rainy Sound

The wind has such a rainy sound,
Moaning through the town,
The sea has such a windy sound,
Will the ships go down?

The apples in the orchard
Tumble from their tree.
Oh will the ships go down, go down,
In the windy sea?

Christina Rossetti

A Toadstool Comes up in a Night

A toadstool comes up in a night,
Learn the lesson, little folk:
An oak grows on a hundred years,
But then it is an oak.

Christina Rossetti

Hospitality

Said a Snake to a Frog with a wrinkled skin,
"As I notice, dear, that your dress is thin,
And a rain is coming, I'll take you in."

John Bannister Tabb

The Dog

Here is the Dog. Since time began,
The Dog has been the friend of man,
The Dog loves man because he shears
His coat and clips his tail and ears.
Man loves the Dog because he'll stay
And listen to his talk all day,
And wag his tail and show delight
At all his jokes, however trite.
His bark is far worse than his bite,
So people say. They may be right;
Yet if to make a choice I had,
I'd choose his bark, however bad.

Oliver Herford

Donkey

If I had a donkey that wouldn't go,
Would I beat him? Oh, no, no.
I'd put him in the barn and give him some corn.
The best little donkey that ever was born.

Anonymous

Swan

Swan swam over the sea;
Swim, swan, swim.
Swan swam back again;
Well swum swan.

Anonymous

This poem is a tricky tongue twister – try saying it out loud.

Seal Lullaby

Oh! Hush thee, my baby, the night is behind us,
And black are the waters that sparkled so green.
The moon, o'er the combers, looks downward to find us
At rest in the hollows that rustle between.
Where billow meets billow, there soft be thy pillow;
Ah, weary wee flipperling, curl at thy ease!
The storm shall not wake thee, nor shark overtake thee,
Asleep in the arms of the slow-swinging seas.

Rudyard Kipling

Combers: big waves

Seals sleep floating just under the water and can come up to breathe without waking up.

From

To a Butterfly

Oh! Pleasant, pleasant were the days,
The time, when, in our childish plays,
My sister Emmeline and I
Together chased the butterfly!
A very hunter did I rush
Upon the prey – with leaps and springs
I followed on from brake to bush;
But she, God love her, feared to brush
The dust from off its wings.

William Wordsworth

Brake: a small clump of trees

Ducks' Ditty

All along the backwater,
Through the rushes tall,
Ducks are a-dabbling,
Up tails all.

Ducks' tails, drakes' tails,
Yellow feet a-quiver,
Yellow bills all out of sight,
Busy in the river!

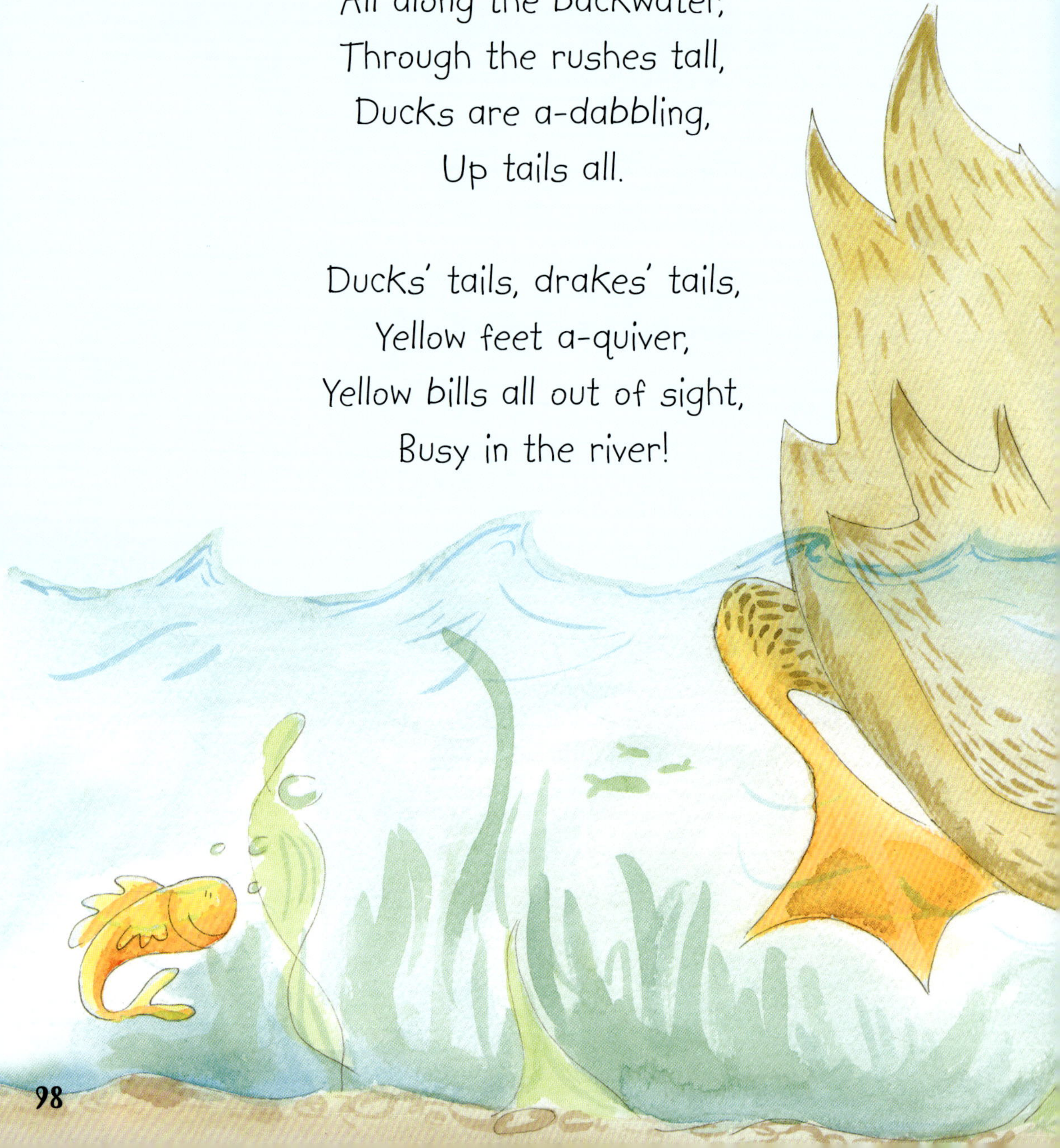

Slushy green undergrowth
Where the roach swim –
Here we keep our larder,
Cool and full and dim.

Everyone for what he likes!
We like to be
Heads down, tails up,
Dabbling free!

High in the blue above
Swifts whirl and call –
We are down a-dabbling,
Up tails all.

Kenneth Grahame

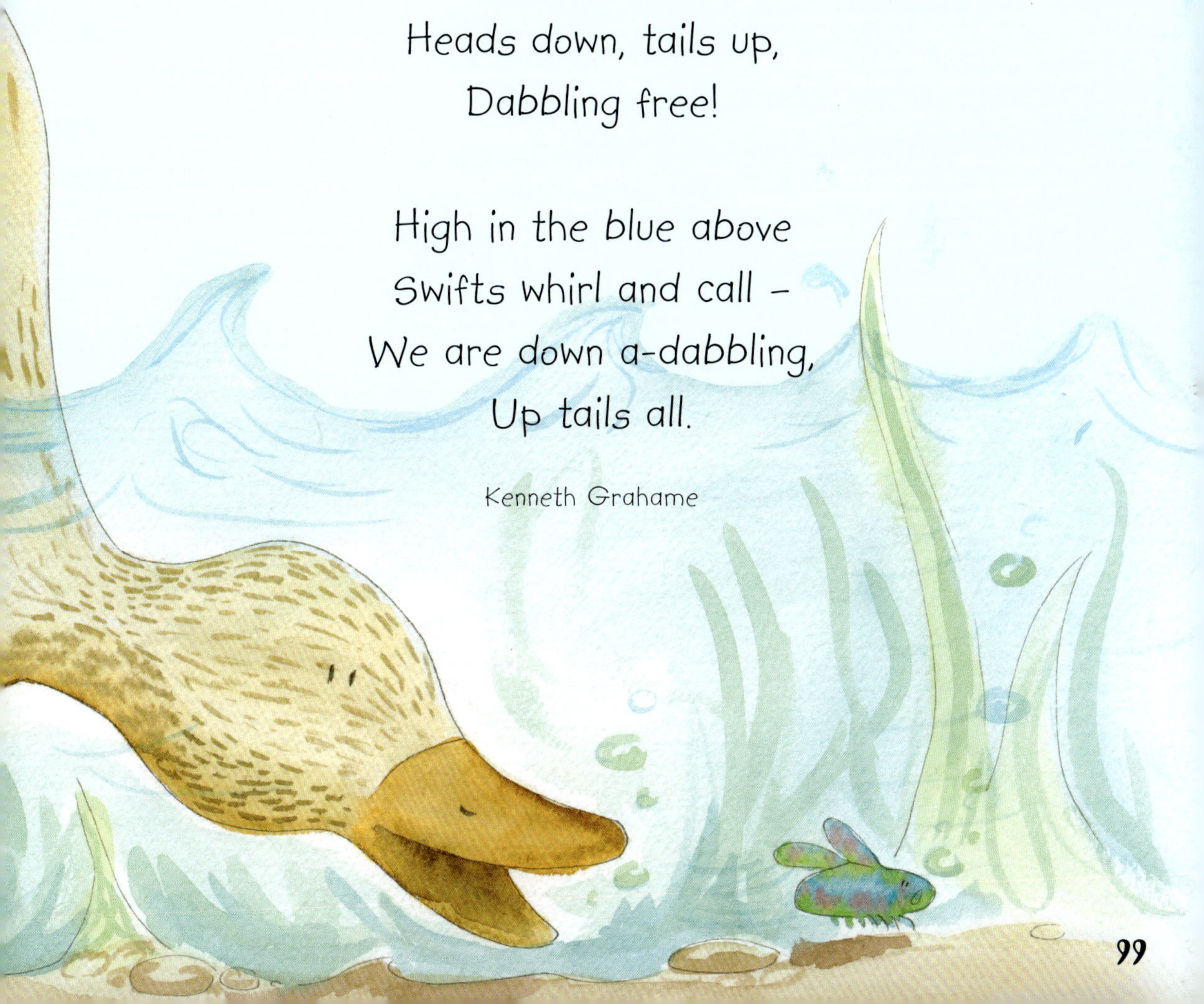

The Snail

The Snail he lives in his hard round house,
In the orchard, under the tree:
Says he, "I have but a single room;
But it's large enough for me."

The snail in his little house doth dwell
All the week from end to end,
You're at home, Master Snail; that's all very well.
But you never receive a friend.

Anonymous

February Twilight

I stood beside a hill
Smooth with new-laid snow,
A single star looked out
From the cold evening glow.
There was no other creature
That saw what I could see –
I stood and watched the evening star
As long as it watched me.

Sara Teasdale

Squirrel

Whisky Frisky,
Hippity hop,
Up he goes
To the tree-top!

Whirly, twirly,
Round and round,
Down he scampers
To the ground.

Furly, curly,
What a tail!
Tall as a feather,
Broad as a sail!

Where's his supper?
In the shell,
Snappy, cracky,
Out it fell!

Anonymous

To a Squirrel at Kyle-Na-No

Come play with me;
Why should you run
Through the shaking tree
As though I'd a gun
To strike you dead?
When all I would do
Is to scratch your head
And let you go.

W B Yeats

Kitten's Complaint

In Winter when the air is chill,
And winds are blowing loud and shrill,
All snug and warm I sit and purr,
Wrapped in my overcoat of fur.
In Summer quite the other way,
I find it very hot all day,
But Human People do not care,
For they have nice thin clothes to wear.
And does it not seem hard to you,
When all the world is like a stew,
And I am much too warm to purr,
I have to wear my Winter Fur?

Oliver Herford

I am his Highness' Dog

I am his Highness' dog at Kew;
Pray tell me sir, whose dog are you?

Alexander Pope

Alexander Pope wrote this poem when the Prince Regent, son of King George III, asked him for a poem for his dog's collar.

My Heart's in the Highlands

My heart's in the Highlands, my heart is not here;
My heart's in the Highlands a-chasing the deer;
Chasing the wild deer, and following the roe,
My heart's in the Highlands wherever I go.
Farewell to the Highlands, farewell to the North,
The birthplace of valour, the country of worth;
Wherever I wander, wherever I rove,
The hills of the Highlands for ever I love.

The Highlands are a beautiful, mountainous region in the far north of Scotland. In this poem, the speaker is remembering the place he loves but has had to leave.

Farewell to the mountains high covered with snow;
Farewell to the straths and green valleys below;
Farewell to the forests and wild hanging woods;
Farewell to the torrents and loud-pouring floods.
My heart's in the Highlands, my heart is not here,
My heart's in the Highlands a-chasing the deer;
Chasing the wild deer, and following the roe,
My heart's in the Highlands wherever I go.

Robert Burns

Strath: a broad valley

What is Pink?

What is pink? A rose is pink
By the fountain's brink.
What is red? A poppy's red
In its barley bed.
What is blue? The sky is blue
Where the clouds float through.
What is white? A swan is white
Sailing in the light.
What is yellow? Pears are yellow,
Rich and ripe and mellow.
What is green? The grass is green,
With small flowers between.
What is violet? Clouds are violet
In the summer twilight.
What is orange? Why, an orange,
Just an orange!

Christina Rossetti

Autumn Greeting

"Come," said the Wind to the Leaves one day.
"Come over the meadow and we will play.
Put on your dresses of red and gold.
For summer is gone and the days grow cold."

Anonymous

The Donkey

I saw a donkey one day old,
His head was too big
for his neck to hold;
His legs were shaky
and long and loose,
They rocked and staggered
and weren't much use.

He tried to gambol
and frisk a bit,
but he wasn't quite sure
of the trick of it.
His queer little coat
was soft and grey
and curled at his neck
in a lovely way.

His face was wistful
and left no doubt
that he felt life needed
some thinking about.
So he blundered round
in venturesome quest,
and then lay flat
on the ground to rest.

He looked so little
and weak and slim,
I prayed the world
might be good to him.

Anonymous

Gambol and frisk: run and jump playfully

The Sea

Behold the wonders
of the deep,
Where crabs and lobsters
learn to creep,
And little fishes
learn to swim,
And clumsy sailors
tumble in.

Anonymous

From

The Starlight Night

Look at the stars! Look, look up at the skies!
O look at all the fire-folk sitting in the air!
The bright boroughs, the circle-citadels there!
Down in dim woods the diamond delves! the elves'-eyes!
The grey lawns cold where gold, where quickgold lies!

Gerard Manley Hopkins

The Wonderful World

Great, wide, beautiful, wonderful World,
With the wonderful water round you curled,
And the wonderful grass upon your breast,
World, you are beautifully dressed.

The wonderful air is over me,
And the wonderful wind is shaking the tree,
It walks on the water, and whirls the mills,
And talks to itself on the top of the hills.

You friendly Earth, how far do you go,
With the wheat fields that nod and the rivers that flow,
With cities and gardens and cliffs and isles,
And the people upon you for thousands of miles?

Wonderful World

Ah! You are so great, and I am so small,
I hardly can think of you, World, at all;
And yet, when I said my prayers today,
My mother kissed me, and said, quite gay,

"If the wonderful world is great to you,
And great to Father and Mother, too,
You are more than the Earth, though you are such a dot!
You can love and think, and the Earth cannot!"

William Brighty Rands

Enchanted Lands

I Asked the Little Boy who Cannot See

I asked the little boy who cannot see,
"And what is colour like?"
"Why, green," said he,
"Is like the rustle when the wind blows through
The forest; running water, that is blue;
And red is like a trumpet sound; and pink
Is like the smell of roses; and I think
That purple must be like a thunderstorm;
And yellow is like something soft and warm;
And white is a pleasant stillness when you lie
And dream."

Anonymous

Meg Merrilies

Old Meg she was a Gipsy,
   And liv'd upon the Moors:
Her bed it was the brown heath turf,
   And her house was out of doors.
Her apples were swart blackberries,
   Her currants pods o' broom;
Her wine was dew of the wild white rose,
   Her book a churchyard tomb.
Her Brothers were the craggy hills,
   Her Sisters larchen trees –
Alone with her great family
   She liv'd as she did please.
No breakfast had she many a morn,
   No dinner many a noon,
And 'stead of supper she would stare
   Full hard against the Moon.

But every morn of woodbine fresh
  She made her garlanding,
And every night the dark glen Yew
  She wove, and she would sing.
And with her fingers old and brown
  She plaited Mats o' Rushes,
And gave them to the Cottagers
  She met among the Bushes.
Old Meg was brave as Margaret Queen
  And tall as Amazon:
An old red blanket cloak she wore;
  A chip hat had she on.
God rest her aged bones somewhere –
  She died full long agone!

John Keats

Garlanding: a flowery ring or wreath
Woodbine: honeysuckle

A Prince

A daring prince, of the realm Rangg Dhune,
Once went up in a big balloon
That caught and stuck on the horns of the moon,
And he hung up there till next day noon –
When all at once he exclaimed, "Hoot-toot!"
And then came down in his parachute.

James Whitcomb Riley

A Fairy in Armour

He put his acorn helmet on;
It was plumed of the silk of
   the thistle down;
The corselet plate that guarded
   his breast
Was once the wild bee's golden vest;
His cloak, of a thousand mingled dyes,
Was formed of the wings of butterflies;
His shield was the shell of a lady-bird green,
Studs of gold on a ground of green;
And the quivering lance which he brandished bright,
Was the sting of a wasp he had slain in fight.

Joseph Rodman Drake

Corselet: armour or piece of armour

Wynken, Blynken and Nod

Wynken, Blynken, and Nod one night
Sailed off in a wooden shoe –
Sailed on river of crystal light,
Into a sea of dew.
"Where are you going, and what do you wish?"
The old moon asked the three.
"We have come to fish for the herring-fish
That live in this beautiful sea;
Nets of silver and gold have we!"
Said Wynken,
Blynken,
And Nod.

The old moon laughed and sang a song,
As they rocked in the wooden shoe,
And the wind that sped them all night long
Ruffled the waves of dew.
The little stars were the herring-fish
That lived in that beautiful sea –
"Now cast your nets wherever you wish
Never afeared are we;"
So cried the stars to the fishermen three:
Wynken,
Blynken,
And Nod.

All night long their nets they threw
  To the stars in the twinkling foam –
Then down from the skies came the wooden shoe,
  Bringing the fishermen home;
'Twas all so pretty a sail, it seemed
  As if it could not be,
And some folks thought 'twas a dream they'd dreamed
  Of sailing that beautiful sea
  But I shall name you the fishermen three:
    Wynken,
    Blynken,
    And Nod.

Wynken and Blynken are two little eyes,
And Nod is a little head,
And the wooden shoe that sailed the skies
Is a wee one's trundle-bed.
So shut your eyes while mother sings
Of wonderful sights that be,
And you shall see the beautiful things
As you rock on the misty sea,
Where the old shoe rocked the fishermen three:
Wynken,
Blynken,
And Nod.

Eugene Field

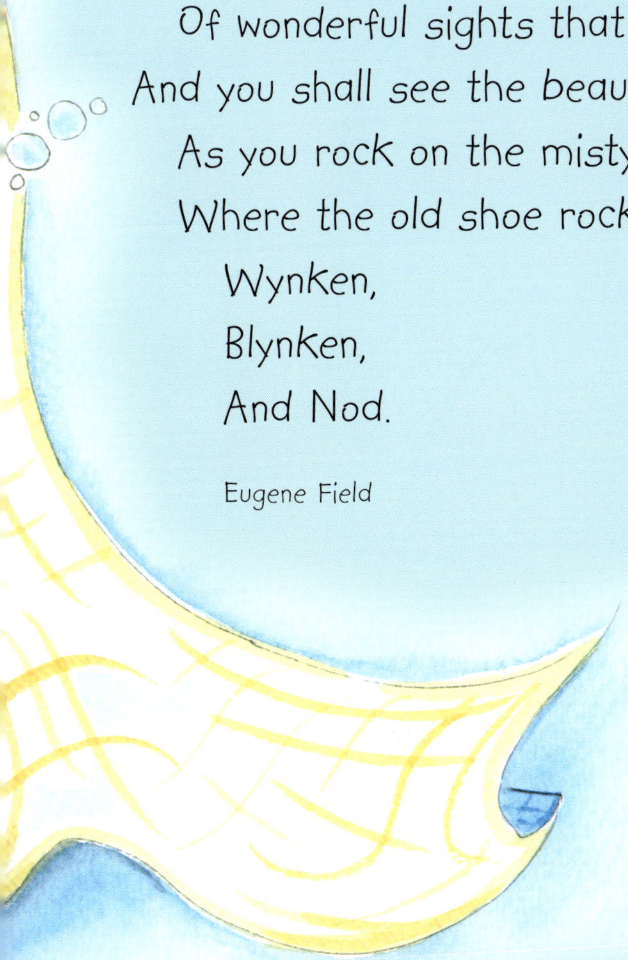

Minnie and Winnie

Minnie and Winnie
Slept in a shell.
Sleep, little ladies!
And they slept well.

Pink was the shell within,
Silver without;
Sounds of the great sea
Wandered about.

Sleep little ladies!
Wake not soon!
Echo on echo
Dies to the moon.

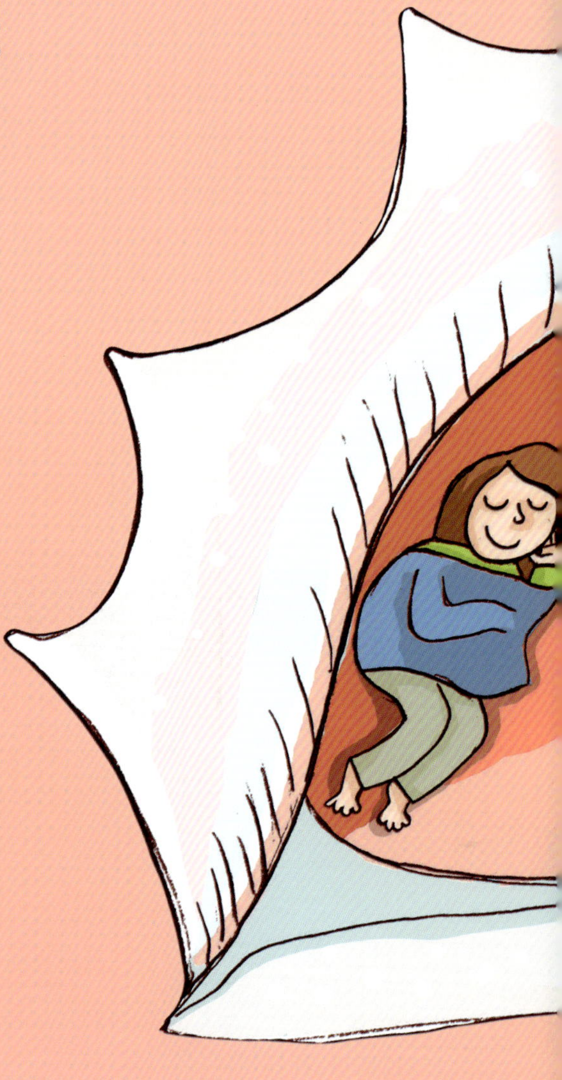

Two bright stars
Peep'd into the shell,
What are they dreaming of?
Who can tell?

Started a green linnet
Out of the croft;
Wake, little ladies,
The sun is aloft!

Alfred, Lord Tennyson

Linnet: a common small bird
Croft: a small farm building

The Owl

When cats run home and light is come,
And dew is cold upon the ground,
And the far-off stream is dumb,
And the whirring sail goes round;
And the whirring sail goes round;
Alone and warming his five wits,
The white owl in the belfry sits.

When merry milkmaids click the latch,
And rarely smells the new-mown hay,
And the cock hath sung beneath the thatch
Twice or thrice his roundelay,
Twice or thrice his roundelay;
Alone and warming his five wits,
The white owl in the belfry sits.

Alfred, Lord Tennyson

Belfry: bell tower
Roundelay: a type of song that repeats itself

A Witch's Spell

Fillet of a fenny snake,
In the cauldron boil and bake;
Eye of newt, and toe of frog,
Wool of bat, and tongue of dog,

Adder's fork, and blind-worm's sting,
Lizard's leg, and howlet's wing,
For a charm of powerful trouble,
Like a hell-broth boil and bubble.

Double, double toil and trouble;
Fire burn and cauldron bubble...

Cool it with a baboon's blood
Now the spell is thick and good.

William Shakespeare

Fenny: marshy
Howlet: owl or owlet

A Fairy's Song

Where the bee sucks, there suck I;
In the cowslip's bell I lie;
There I couch when owls do cry
On the bat's back I do fly
After summer, merrily:
Merrily, merrily shall I live now,
Under the blossom that hangs on the bough.

William Shakespeare

Couch: lie

Terence McDiddler

Terence McDiddler,
The three-stringed fiddler,
Can charm, if you please,
The fish from the seas.

Anonymous

The Land of Counterpane

When I was sick and lay a-bed,
I had two pillows at my head,
And all my toys beside me lay
To keep me happy all the day.

And sometimes for an hour or so
I watched my leaden soldiers go,
With different uniforms and drills,
Among the bed clothes,
 through the hills;

And sometimes sent my ships in fleets
All up and down among the sheets;
Or brought my trees and houses out,
And planted cities all about.

I was the giant great and still
That sits upon the pillow-hill,
And sees before him, dale and plain,
The pleasant land of counterpane.

Robert Louis Stevenson

Counterpane: a bedspread

Climbing

High up in the apple tree climbing I go,
With the sky above me, the Earth below.
Each branch is the step of a wonderful stair
Which leads to the town I see shining up there.

Climbing, climbing, higher and higher,
The branches blow and I see a spire,
The gleam of a turret, the glint of a dome,
All sparkling and bright, like white sea foam.

On and on, from bough to bough,
The leaves are thick, but I push my way through;
Before, I have always had to stop,
But today I am sure I shall reach the top.

Today to the end of the marvellous stair,
Where those glittering pinacles flash in the air!
Climbing, climbing, higher I go,
With the sky close above me, the earth far below.

Amy Lowell

The Elf and the Dormouse

Under a toadstool crept a wee Elf,
Out of the rain to shelter himself.

Under the toadstool, sound asleep,
Sat a big Dormouse all in a heap.

Trembled the wee Elf, frightened and yet
Fearing to fly away lest he get wet.

To the next shelter – maybe a mile!
Sudden the wee Elf smiled a wee smile.

Tugged till the toadstool toppled in two.
Holding it over him, gaily he flew.

Soon he was safe home, dry as could be.
Soon woke the Dormouse – "Good gracious me!"

"Where is my toadstool?" loud he lamented.
– And that's how umbrellas first were invented.

Oliver Herford

Nine Little Goblins

They all climbed up on a high board-fence,
Nine little Goblins that had no sense,
Nine little Goblins, with green-glass eyes,
And couldn't tell coppers from cold mince pies;
And they all climbed up on the fence, and sat,
And I asked them what they were staring at.

And the first one said, as he
scratched his head
With a queer little arm that
reached out of his ear
And rasped its claws in his hair
so red,
"This is what this little arm is for!"
And he scratched and stared,
and the next one said,
"How on earth do you scratch
your head?"

And he laughed like the screech
of a rusty hinge,
Laughed and laughed till his
face grew black;
And when he clicked, with
a final twinge
Of his stifling laughter, he thumped his back
With a fist that grew on the end of his tail
Till the breath came back to his lips so pale.

And the third little Goblin leered round at me,
And there were no lids on his eyes at all
And he clucked one eye, and he says, says he,
"What is the style of your socks this fall?"
And he clapped his heels and I sighed to see
That he had hands where his feet should be.

Then a bald-faced Goblin, grey and grim,
Bowed his head, and I saw him slip
His eyebrows off, as I looked at him,
And paste them over his upper lip;
And then he moaned in remorseful pain,
"Would, ah, would I'd me brows again!"

And then the whole of the Goblin band
Rocked on the fence-top to and fro,
And clung, in a long row, hand in hand,
Singing the songs that they used to know,
Singing the songs that their grandsires sung
In the goo-goo days of the Goblin-tongue.

And ever they kept their green-glass eyes
Fixed on me with a stony stare,
Till my own grew glazed with a dread surmise,
And my hat whooped up on my lifted hair,
And I felt the heart in my breast snap to
As you've heard the lid of a snuff box do.

And they sang "You're asleep! There is no board-fence,
And never a Goblin with green-glass eyes!
"'Tis only a vision the mind invents
After a supper of cold mince pies,
And you're doomed to dream this way," they said,
"And you shan't wake up till you're clean plumb dead!"

James Whitcomb Riley

From

The Mermaid

Who would be
A mermaid fair,
Singing alone,
Combing her hair
Under the sea,
In a golden curl
With a comb of pearl,
On a throne?

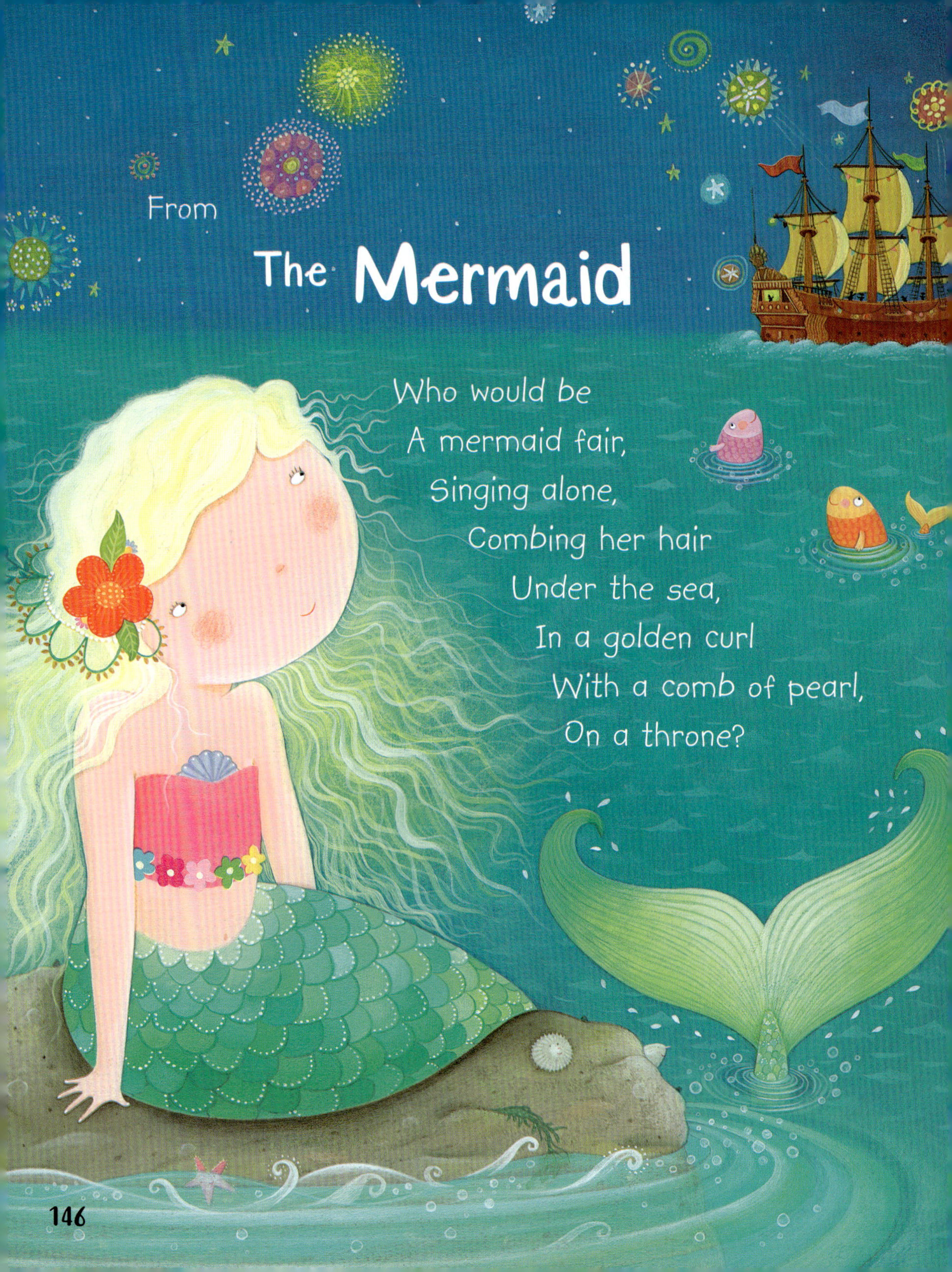

I would be a mermaid fair;
I would sing to myself the whole of the day;
With a comb of pearl I would comb my hair;
And still as I comb'd I would sing and say,
Who is it loves me? who loves not me?
I would comb my hair till my ringlets would fall
Low adown, low adown,
From under my starry sea-bud crown
Low adown and around,
And I should look like a fountain of gold
Springing alone
With a shrill inner sound,
Over the throne
In the midst of the hall;
And all the mermen under the sea
Would feel their immortality
Die in their hearts for the love of me.

Alfred, Lord Tennyson

From

The Gipsies

The fairy beam upon you,
The stars to glisten on you,
A moon of light
In the noon of night,
Till the firedrake hath o'er-gone you.
The wheel of fortune guide you,
The boy with the bow beside you
Run aye in the way
Till the bird of day
And the luckier lot betide you.

Ben Jonson

Aye: always
Betide: you come to you
Firedrake: will-o'-the-wisp, a light that dances above marshes, caused by a form of natural gas

Nonsense

I had a boat, and the boat had wings;
And I did dream that we went a flying
Over the heads of queens and kings,
Over the souls of dead and dying,
Up among the stars and the great white rings,
And where the Moon on her back is lying.

Mary Coleridge

The Elves' Goodbye

The moonlight fades from flower and tree,
And the stars dim one by one;
The tale is told, the song is sung,
And the Fairy feast is done.
The night-wind rocks the sleeping flowers,
And sings to them, soft and low.
The early birds erelong will wake –
'Tis time for the Elves to go.

O'er the sleeping earth we silently pass,
Unseen by mortal eye,
And send sweet dreams, as we lightly float
Through the quiet moonlit sky;
For the stars' soft eyes alone may see,
And the flowers alone may know,
The feasts we hold, the tales we tell –
So 'tis time for the Elves to go.

From bird, and blossom, and bee,
We learn the lessons they teach;
And seek, by kindly deeds, to win
A loving friend in each.
And though unseen on earth we dwell,
Sweet voices whisper low,
And gentle hearts most joyously greet
The Elves where'er they go.

When next we meet in the Fairy dell,
May the silver moon's soft light
Shine then on faces gay as now,
And Elfin hearts as light.
Now spread each wing, for the eastern sky
With sunlight soon will glow.
The morning star shall light us home –
Farewell! For the Elves must go.

Louisa M Alcott

Sea Shell

Sea Shell, Sea Shell,
Sing me a song, O Please!
A song of ships, and sailor men,
And parrots, and tropical trees,
Of islands lost in the Spanish Main
Which no man ever may find again,
Of fishes and corals under the waves,
And seahorses stabled in great green caves.
Sea Shell, Sea Shell,
Sing of the things you know so well.

Amy Lowell

Once

Once I was a monarch's daughter,
And sat on a lady's knee;
But am now a nightly rover,
Banished to the ivy tree.

Crying hoo, hoo, hoo, hoo, hoo, hoo,
Hoo, hoo, hoo, My feet are cold.
Pity me, for here you see me
Persecuted, poor, and old.

Hoolet: an owl or baby owl

I once was a king's daughter
And sat on my father's knee
But now I'm a poor hoolet
And hide in a hollow tree.

Anonymous

Index of Poets

Index of First Lines